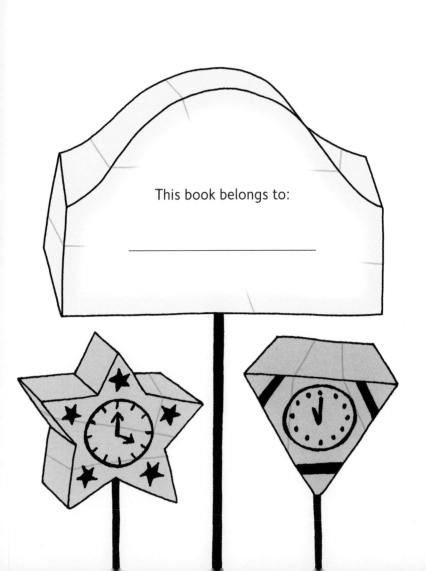

This book belongs to:

_____

Nick Sharratt

Carnival of the Clocks

Barrington Stoke

First published in 2022 in Great Britain by
Barrington Stoke Ltd
18 Walker Street, Edinburgh, EH3 7LP

www.barringtonstoke.co.uk

Text & Illustrations © 2022 Nick Sharratt

A CIP catalogue record for this book is available
from the British Library upon request

ISBN: 978-1-80090-128-5

Printed by Hussar Books, Poland

This book is in a super-readable format for young readers
beginning their independent reading journey.

*This book is dedicated to
Same Sky and the children
of Brighton and Hove*

It's a dark winter's evening.

Lessons finished long ago.

And something odd is going on in the playground ...

Everywhere you look
there are clocks.

Round clocks,

square clocks,

triangular clocks.

Pentagonal clocks,

hexagonal clocks,

octagonal clocks.

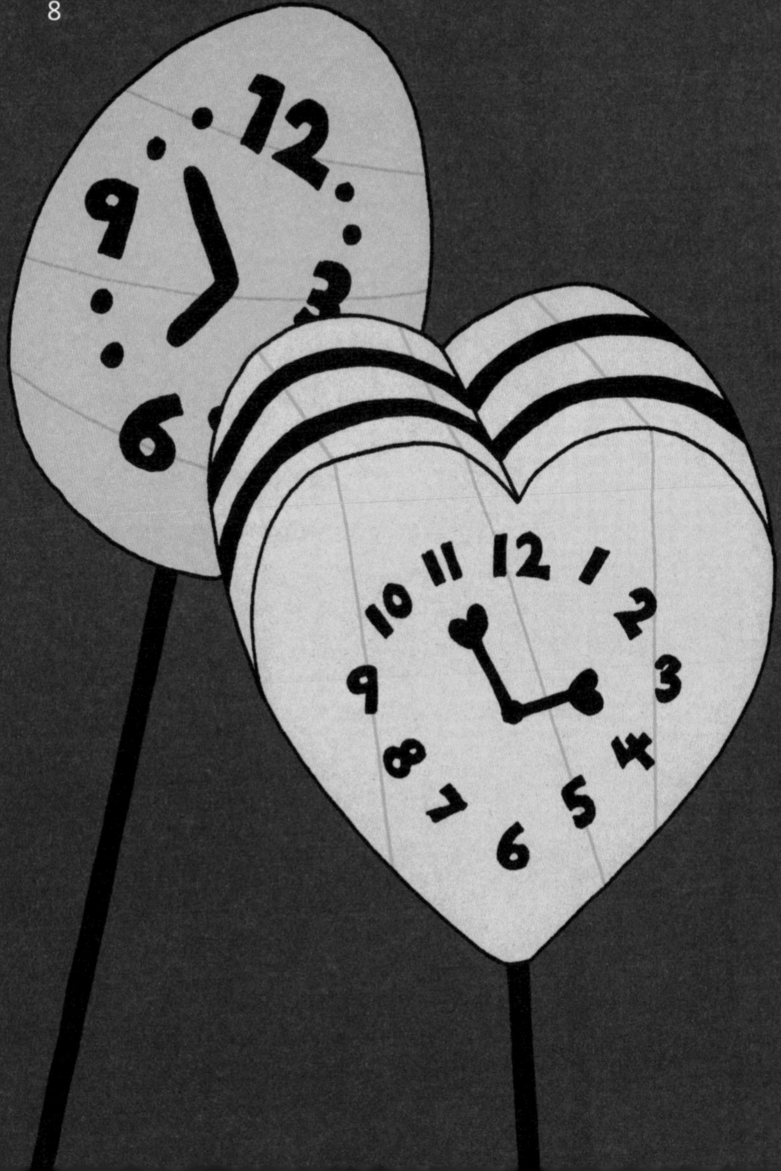

Egg-shaped clocks,
heart-shaped clocks,
star-shaped clocks.

But look closely.

They're not clocks – they're lanterns.

Class One are in the playground and they've all got clock-shaped lanterns!

Soraya has
a simple
clock lantern.

Freya has a
fancy clock
lantern.

Abdullah has
an alarm clock
lantern.

Cole has a
cuckoo clock
lantern.

Grace has a
grandfather
clock lantern.

Dev has a dinosaur clock lantern.

Summer's clock lantern says
six o'clock.

Toby's clock
lantern says
two o'clock.

Amelie's clock lantern says half past eight.

Stanley's clock lantern says quarter past seven.

Tod's clock lantern says
twenty to twelve.

And Tallulah's clock lantern
says twenty-one fifty.

Why are all of Class One holding
lanterns shaped like clocks?

WHAT'S GOING ON?

Well ... do you know what day it is today?

It's the 21st of December – the shortest day of the year.

SUN	MON	TUE	WED	THU	FRI	SAT
				1	2	3
4	5	6	7	8	9	10
11	12	13	14	15	16	17
18	19	20	21	22	23	24
25	26	27	28	29	30	31

From now on the days will gradually be getting longer and it won't be dark so early.

Every year, to celebrate this special day, the children of the town make clock lanterns (with a little help from the grown-ups).

They make them in all shapes and sizes, from willow sticks and tissue paper.

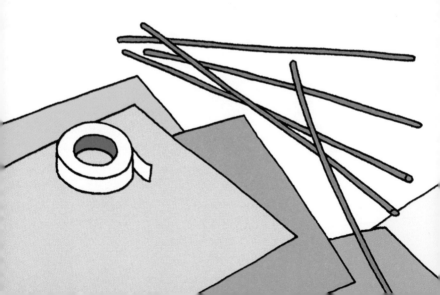

They decorate them, put lights inside them and attach them to poles.

And when darkness falls on the shortest day, the children parade through the town with their clock lanterns.

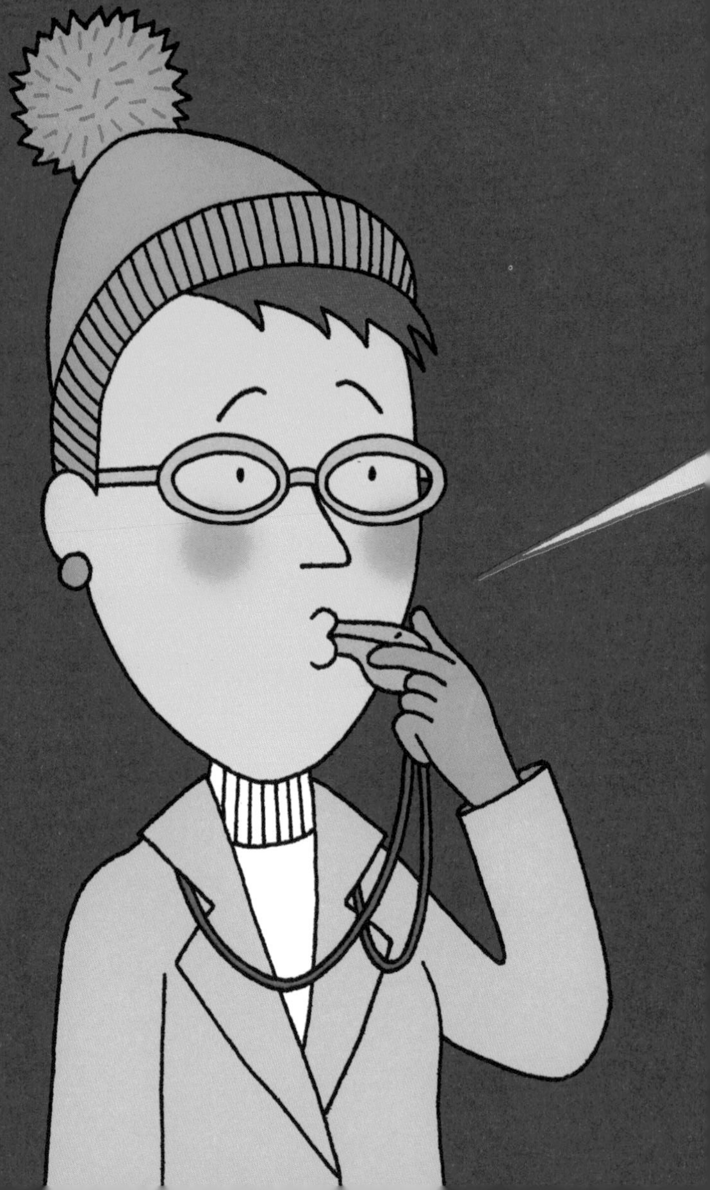

PEEEEEEEEEEEP!

In the playground Mrs Thistle
blows her whistle.

"It's time to join the procession!"
she says.

Class One and the teachers head off to join the other schools.

They can hear the sound of drumming.

RAT-A-TAT TAT! RAT-A-TAT TAT!

The drummers lead the way.
They march past the shops
and cafes.

They march past
the theatre.

They march past the town hall and down to the seafront.

They march past the big hotels

34

35

and the beach huts

and the boats.

They march
past the pier.

They march down to the beach.

And that's where they stop.

Up above them, Class One can see their
mums and their dads and their carers,
their brothers and sisters, their aunties

and uncles and cousins, their grannies
and grandads, their friends and their
neighbours, all watching and waving.

The lights are taken out
of the lanterns and they're
passed along and piled up
by the grown-ups into a
huge lantern mountain.

There's a big countdown.

TEN!

NINE!

EIGHT!

SEVEN!

SIX!

FIVE!

FOUR!

THREE!

TWO!

ONE!

The lantern mountain is set alight. In a flash it becomes a roaring bonfire.

Flames leap into the dark.

Fireworks fill the sky.

WHIZZZ! BANG! FIZZZ!

Class One cheer and shout
with all the other children.

HOORAY FOR THE

This book was inspired by the annual
Burning the Clocks event, created by
the community arts charity Same Sky,
and taking place in Brighton on
the 21st of December.

Our books are tested
for children and young people by
children and young people.

Thanks to everyone who consulted on
a manuscript for their time and effort in
helping us to make our books better
for our readers.